If You Want to See a Caribou

PHYLLIS ROOT

ILLUSTRATED BY **JIM MEYER**

BIG-LEAF ASTER

Houghton Mifflin Company Boston 2004

www.houghtonmifflinbooks.com

The text of this book is set in Legacy Serif Medium.
The illustrations are woodblock prints.

Library of Congress Cataloging-in-Publication Data
Root, Phyllis.
If you want to see a caribou / by Phyllis Root ; illustrated by Jim
Meyer.
p. cm.
Summary: Describes all the wonders of nature that the reader might
see when setting out to find a caribou on an island in Lake Superior.
ISBN 0-618-39314-5
[1. Caribou—Fiction. 2. Lake Superior region—Fiction.] I. Title.
PZ7.R6784If 2004   [E]—dc22   2003012291

Printed in Singapore
TWP 10 9 8 7 6 5 4 3 2 1

THIMBLEBERRY

For fellow sailors, Doug and Susan and Mark and Mary and especially Robert, who knows all the names.
—P. R.

For Amanda, Brady, Jordan, Alyssa, Jamie, Joey, Jessica, Luke, Josh, Jake, and all the JEMs.
—J. M.

BUTTERCUP

If you want to see a caribou,

you must go to a place where the caribou live.

You might go by boat on a good sailing day

to an island in Lake Superior,

the wind curving your sails,

the waves rushing, *rooosh, rooosh.*

You might sail into a bay

cupped by rocky green hills

and drop anchor in quiet water.

Somewhere a loon calls, high and wild.

If you want to see a caribou,

you might go ashore and follow the trails

churned black by caribou hooves.

Spruce trees tower over you.

You stoop under branches

draped with old-man's-beard lichen,

wade through tiny meadows of pearly everlasting.

Yellow buttercups nod, *hello, hello*.

You might step over birch logs,

bark peeling, green with pixie cups.

If a log is pointed like a pencil,

you will know that a beaver gnawed down a tree

too huge to haul away.

If you want to see a caribou, you might follow those trails,

soft with rain,

through stands of balsams.

Needles brush you with their scent.

You might come to the heart of the woods,

the light falling green,

the ground spongy with feather moss.

Pale Indian pipes poke up

by the moss-edged bones of a caribou long dead.

Then you will know that you are close.

Or perhaps you come to a clearing

with stripped, stubby pines

where caribou have rubbed the velvet off their antlers

and the air has a faint, acrid odor.

Under fallen maple branches,

where caribou cannot reach,

big-leaf asters and thimbleberries grow.

You might find a yellow flicker feather at your feet.

Caribou eyes may be watching you,

but you might not see a caribou.

So you follow the trail on,

down to the water's edge again,

down to a shelf of rock where you sit,

quiet as an old spruce is quiet,

quiet as a red cupped mushroom,

quiet as a caribou who scents danger on the wind.

Quiet enough that two beavers swim nearby in silver vees, diving for waterweed to stuff in their mouths.

If you are quiet,
and if you wait,
the caribou may come.
Cow and calf,
long-legged, white-ankled, gangly,
wading with awkward grace,
the young calf gawking behind,
then splashing ahead.

And if you are silent, watching still,

the caribou may browse

so close that when you whisper your name,

the caribou calf flicks his ears

before he follows his mother into the forest

and is gone.

Evening may be coming on,

so you make your way back to your sailboat home,

walking quiet as a caribou walks,

knowing

you have seen a caribou.

And a caribou knows your name.

WOODLAND CARIBOU

If you want to see a caribou, you might have a very difficult time. Places where you can see woodland caribou are vanishing. Once these caribou lived in evergreen forests over much of northern North America. Today, mostly because of human activity and loss of habitat, woodland caribou are endangered in the United States and threatened (which is one step from being endangered) in Canada.

In Canada in the early 1900s a herd of woodland caribou, like the ones in this story, crossed over the ice of Lake Superior in a rare winter when the lake froze. These caribou have lived ever since on a group of islands. Caribou are good swimmers and often swim from island to island, but the mainland is too far for them to swim back. Because no predators crossed over the ice with the caribou, and because the government protects the islands, these caribou have thrived, eating the lichens, moss, fungi, twigs, grass, leaves, and plants growing on the islands.